Molested With Malice

By

Dana N Frazier & Derrick L Henderson Jr.

Table of Contents

CHAPTER 1

"Let me out! Let me out! My mind, my soul... I have no control. Where am I? Who am I? I'm lost, confused, stuck in chaos. "

He wakes up in a dark world with cold rain pouring around him. Hearing guns firing, he screams in agony, then takes off running through the cold air. He's dressed all in black, with a cape-like cloak around his neck and shoulders, his heart beats fast and his mind is constantly racing.

The running doesn't stop until he trips over something that was stuck in the mud. It was a pointy, medium sized object, black like a stick or wand of some sorts. He grabs it immediately, as if he recognizes it. He instantly notices his surroundings. He's in some type of graveyard, there are tombstones all around him. It sends chills down his spine. He knows where he is. Then he turns around to hear two loud popping noises followed by a loud voice.

"Where the hell do you think you're going? Your soul belongs to us now! We own you."

Another man comes up behind him. He pulls him away and grabs the pointy stick figure, mumbling nonsense.

"yadyreve yad lla detavitom cisum..."

"He will be reborn! He will be back for his throne!"

Red smoke appears in front of him instantly turning into blood.

Four men grabbed him and pulled him into total darkness.

The bell rings. Devon Gates Smith lifts his head up and realizes he slept over his entire sixth period history class. He notices that everyone was leaving the room and wipes his slobber off his face but his teacher stands in front of him and says:

"Devon, you better get it together. The very important OGT test are in less than two months and you're failing my class. You still need to pass your history, math and science portion of the test. Those tests are very important. You cannot graduate without them."

"Yeah. I know." Devon said. "I have already taken them all multiple times since my 10th grade year and I've only been able to manage to pass the writing and reading but that's okay. Mr. Geiger, I am definitely walking the stage with my class."

Devon then darts out the class into the hallway and thinks to himself.

"At least I hope I walk the stage with everyone." He moved rapidly down the hallway to his locker when he noticed the second bell rings, which is the bell that warns students that they had about two minutes left before the next class begins. He grabs his coat and slams his locker.

"Fuck this. I'm out of here for the day. "

He throws his book bag over his shoulders and starts to walk towards the nearest exit. He would use every opportunity to flick school, once he stepped outside he`s hit by a slight breeze.

The sun was out. It was February and the snow melted from the past weekend, when it had been so cold - with about 4 inches of snow on the ground.

Devon zipped up his coat and was getting ready to take off down the walkway when someone grabbed his shoulders.

"Why aren't you in class?"

Devon spun around to see it wasn't nobody but one of his classmates that everybody called Randy although his real name was Randall.

"You trying to smoke?"

Devon paused, thought about it for a minute and said:

" Why not? "

"Okay. Cool. Randy said:

" We just got to walk to the store and grab some swishers."

Swishers were a form of paper to wrap their marijuana in. They then walked to the nearest corner store, which was actually in the school vicinity. It's what tempted students to flick so often because you could go grab a snack before your next class or even dip out for lunch. As they walked through the 45-degree breezy day, Devon asked Randy:

"What's been up with you?"

Randy replied:

"Shit! Just ready for this corny school year to be over." Devon agreed.

"I feel that." then he asked Randy. "How did you do on your OGT Test?"

"Those test are stupid." Randy stated

"I haven't passed any of them yet. It's aggravating, but it's cool."

" Forget school dude let`s get high"

They arrived at the corner store, a store that was very famous for being open a good 25 to 30 plus years. They walked in the store. It was pretty much dead this time of day. Randy went straight to the front register and Devon went to the aisle to grab his favorite potato chips: honey barbecue.

He snatched them off the shelf and headed back to the front register to Randy who grabbed Devon by the arm, whispering:

"Dude, he won't let me get it without my ID." Devon paid for his chips and they walked out of the store. Someone approached them . It was a girl with blonde dyed hair, caramel complexion, tight light blue jeans and a pair of jordan tennis shoes. It seemed she had just hopped out of a car that just pulled up in front of the store. Randy spoke quickly.

"Hey Ma. What's up? You trying to match them up?"

She smiled and said it:

"Depends. What yaw'l smoking on?"

"No doubt. I got a dime of this cushy smoke, we can all blow fair. You just got to get us a swisher."

She said: "Cool."

Then went into the store and came back out within a couple minutes and said:" here you go" tossing the pack of Swisher's to Randy.

"Y'all riding with us?"

She asked and pointed to the all black dodge charger sitting in front of the store parking lot.

Devon looked at Randy and said:

"Are you sure? We don't know them all like that?"

He said "hell, yeah, we about to smoke so good" as they went over to enter the car. Devon noticed the license plate read:" Dope boy trap star" as they hopped in the backseat of the vehicle. There was a dark-skinned girl with a head scarf on her head, talking on the phone in the driver seat.

Seeing them, she hung up the phone and turned to her friend :

" Rhonda, uh-huh. Who are these dudes? You got in my car!" Rhonda responded

"Chill. They about to smoke with us. " The girl in the driver seat then got calm and turned to the back seat.

" Hey! Im Ebony."

"What's up with y'all two?" Randy spoke first.

"Nothing much, about to smoke on this good kush."

" It better be some good shit. I've been depressed lately, but aren't you two supposed to be in school?"

Devon spoke for the first time since being in the vehicle.

"Yeah, but we're not worried about that. Now we trying to blaze up."

Ebony laughed and started backing the car out of the store parking lot.

Devon asked:

"Where are we going? "

Ronda answered:

" We can chill at my people`s house for a bit. I got the keys and they are not home. they all cruised through

the neighborhood with Ebony's music blasting loudly. It took them all of seven minutes or so and they were pulling up a double driveway on the side of a tall light blue house that had a humongous backyard. Randy hopped out the car first and said:

" Devon, we can have a class football game back here."

They laughed, the two girls chuckled and started walking to the side door of the house.

Devon grabbed Randy by the shirt and said: " Dude how long are we staying over here? I forgot I was supposed to go straight home after school."

"Chill, bro. I'll get you back there. We don't want you to get punished again. "

Randy then smirked at him as they entered the side door going into the house. They could already hear music playing above them. They walked past the basement steps and up a two step landing that led them right through a kitchen.

It was dirty from top to bottom: dishes in the sink, trash on the floor, empty cans added a very funky smell to it . And that was just the kitchen. . They didn't like the living room either but that's where the girls were sitting on sofas watching a 40 inch flat screen TV. Rhonda told the two boys:

" Y'all come in and chill and roll some of that weed up."

They sat down on the couch next to the girls and looked up at the TV. The girls were watching MTV Jams music videos at that moment.

Devon looked at the screen and noticed a really weird feeling when he looked at the TV show.

His heart started beating fast and head started pounding. "What is wrong with me?" He thought to himself. "I haven't even started smoking yet." He shook the feeling off and took his phone out and started looking at it. "Well, it's 2:30 right now. We should be able to make it back before it gets too late." He thought, to himself then he looked at Rhonda asked her:

"Where is the bathroom?" She answered:

"First door on the right, up the stairs."

He hopped up and steadily, walked up the staircase, when he reached the bathroom and walked in, he started thinking: "This is worse than the kitchen."

There was dirty laundry all over the floor that hadn't been moved in a while. The tub had dirt in it and looked as if it was never washed. or no one cleaned the place for several months, even the toilet wasn't flushed. It also had shit floating in it, which you could smell as soon as you approached the door. Devon flushed the toilet and it seemed to be clogged and backed up.

He turned his face down in disgust.

"Fuck this. I'll just piss outside."

He then turned to the sink and pulled down the lever on the knob and cold water came splashing out of the faucet. He looked in the mirror at his reflection and thought: "Why was I feeling like that when I was downstairs ? It seemed to happen when I looked at the TV. Oh, well! " He shrugged and splashed two hands full of water on his face.

Once he returned to the living room, the group were already smoking. Randy called for Devon as he reached the bottom step.

" Hey, come get in rotation."

"This shit hitting good."

 Devon plopped down on the couch next to Randy. He stared at the two girls. They seem to be chatting about the new show. He noticed the Channel had been changed to a show called "Maury" where a host does a lie detector test to determine if someone's cheating on their spouse or significant other, live. "The show is full of heavy drama" - Devon notices. He didn't have the same feeling he had earlier watching that other show. Randy tapped him on the shoulder and said:

"Here, chief. Smoke away."

Devon took the blunt and took a good inhale of the smoke and instantly exhaled it deeply and started coughing vigorously and loudly. The two girls and Randy started laughing. Rhonda said:

"Slow down man. You took a good hit of that, didn't you? "

After they smoked about four blunts, time went by fast and it was now about 10 minutes after 6:00. Devon hadn't realized how late it was getting but due to all the smoking he didn't check the time until now.

He was ready to leave but Randy was actually slumped over and dozed off sleep.. Devon did feel drowsy himself, but he shook it off and was about to speak when Ebony loudly stated:

"Everybody be quiet! My show is about to start!"

She turned on a music show on channel B.E.T. It was called "106 & Park" and it displayed the month's hottest industry music videos. Ebony and Rhonda started talking about all the artists that were going to be on the show on that day.

When the number 10 video of the countdown came on the screen, suddenly, out of nowhere, there it was again: the same feeling Devon had felt earlier. This one a little bit more intense, as if he was stuck in some form of trance. He tried standing; his legs were shaking, his head pounding like the beat of a drum. He shut his eyes for a moment trying to shake it off. It didn't work. He opened them back up and looked at Ebony and said:

"Hey do you mind turning the volume down a bit?"

She was just about to respond when her phone started ringing. She answered it right away. You could hear a loud dude on the other end, yelling so she yelled back at him.

"Well, fuck you too!" She hung up with a lot of anger in her voice. "We got to go, my baby's daddy is on the rampage again."

Rhonda looked nervous judging by the expression in her face. She asked her friend:

"Does he know where you are?"

"Yes, and he's on his way here."

Devon shook Randy.

"Wake up dude. Did you know she had a baby dad?" He answered in a sarcastic tone:

"No but what girl doesn't have one these days?"

"Well, she said he was on his way to get her. So we got to go." Randy pouted for a minute and said:

"Alright, let's go."

They got their things together, turned everything off and rushed towards the kitchen

Devon could only wonder why there was a strange urgency to leave so quickly but the boys followed anyway, once they got outside, on the side of the house Rhonda locked the door.

They all hopped in the car and Randy spoke up

"Well you can drop us back off at the corner store." Ebony then turned in fear.

"I don't think it's going to be enough time for that."

"What do you mean? " Devon said back to her.

Before he got an answer, a silver and blue vehicle pulled up in the driveway blocking their route to the street.

"Who is that?"Rhonda demanded. The question was answered quickly when a heavyset, tall light-skinned dude got out from the passenger side of the vehicle and started walking right towards them. Ebony spoke first.

"That's my baby's dad."

Once he got close to the car, you could see he had an angry expression on his face. He went straight to Ebony`s driver seat, angrily pulled the door open and said:

"Get the fuck out of my car, stupid bitch."

While grabbing her arm and pretty much throwing her out the front driver seat, he plumped down loudly in to the driver seat, then turned around and said:

"What do you think you're doing? Get your ass in the back, he looked at Rhonda, she smacked her lips. "Got out then got in the backseat and slid in next to Devon and Randy.

"Who are these two young cornball niggas?"

The heavy set dude demanded Devon, looked at Randy only to see if he would speak. Devon was shocked because it was the first time he ever saw Randy speechless. A couple of seconds passed and no one was saying anything. Devon spoke up and said:

" Shit bro, me and my homie... We're just chilling , and smoking with these two." He pointed to the girls in the car.

The guy turned to Ebony and said:

"Your dumb ass! You were smoking while you are pregnant with my child. What did I tell you?"

"This is all my fault!" Rhonda intervened. And before she could say another word, the heavy set dude yelled:

"You shut up! You always getting her into some bullshit! Y'all out here whipping my car around and picking up dudes, smoking in my shit."

Randy said something for the first time since all the commotion.

"We didn't smoke in the car. Everything`s cool, me and my boy can just walk from here."

"No, it's good. I'ma drop everybody off. But first I'm gonna go take my baby mom to the house where her pregnant ass should be."

He started the car and sped out the now unblocked driveway immediately. You could smell the burnt rubber as they turned on the street from all the traction. The drive was very awkward. No one said anything.

Devon hadn't realized his phone had completely died. That meant definite trouble because no one could get a hold of him. It took them a little while to get to their new location because they were obviously going all the way across town. As they drove along Devon thought to himself: "That's why the license plate read Dope Boy Trap Star." He had noticed that before they got in the car with the girls earlier that day.

He started looking out the window and noticed the sun was going down. It was getting a little dark out. "I have to get home". He thought to himself. The car ride went on for another several minutes when they made a right turn on a long one way street. You could tell by the condition of the homes and the people around that it was a bad neighborhood.

Randy leaned over Rhonda to get a good look out the car window, then said out loud are:

" We all the way on the bottom of the east side?"

No one answered for a minute. Then Ebony's baby dad turned to the back seat and said with a weird like smirk on his face:

" Hell, yeah ! This is the bottom. You boys are now in my hood."

Once the car got to the far end of the one-way street, they slowed down and began to pull into the driveway of a brown and black, medium sized house, on the left side of the street. They didn't even pull the car all the way up into the driveway when the vehicle came to a complete stop.

The heavy dude yelled at Ebony to get out.

"I need to holler at you upstairs. " Then turned to the back seat and said: "we'll be back". He got out the car, Ebony had a sorrowful face and she looked scared and hesitant, but she got out and followed behind him into the house. Once they were out the car and in the house, Devon looked at Rhonda and said :

"So is this guy going to take and drop us off?"

She had a confused look on her face.

"Sure. He never brought me back to their place before, he usually drops me off along the way." That startled Devon.

"Then why would he have us all the way out here?"

His voice tone grew in intensity. They heard all kinds of screaming and shouting coming from the inside of the house and then you could hear a girl crying screaming.

"No, don't do it. Not again, please!"

Randy jumped

"What is that?"

Rhonda responded:

" It sounds like Ebony."

She had just started to open her door as if she was going to hop out the car when a group of guys with a pit bull on a chain, walked right past the car towards the front porch of the house. The group of guys went to the porch, pulled up a small round medium sized table and three or four of them started playing cards. A couple of guys tossed some money right on the table.

Rhonda looked back at Devon and said:

"Typical dudes! Always willing to sit around and gamble their money away."

Randy was just about to respond when someone instantly opened the back seat door. They all turned to see who it was - one of the dudes that had just arrived with the group popped his head in the car staring right at Rhonda.

"What's up, baby? You can stop being rude, get out of the car and speak. "

Rhonda smacking lips replied:

"What's up Jeff? Why are you always over here? You don't have a job or anything? " The dude grinned and said:

"Hell no, I'm living this trappy life."

She hopped out of the car and gave him a slight hug as they started talking outside the car, you could hear the group of gamblers on the porch getting a little bit louder. Two guys were arguing about something. Devon turned to Randy.

" Man, this shit pissing me off. We need to get on the move. My phone died and I can't get a hold of anyone. What time is it? "

"Dude it's a little after 8:00 or so."

The street lights just came on. Devon turned to look back outside the car and noticed Rhonda and the other guy made their way to the porch next to the other group.

Randy didn't seem to worry. He pulled out the remaining blunt they were smoking earlier at the house.

"Why are you smoking that now?

"Chill, dude, my high was going down from all this sitting and waiting around."

Devon had an angry look on his face. He was going to respond when suddenly, a lean guy wearing black clothes came to the driver's side of the car, opened the door, got in and sat down. He turned to the back seat and said:

"What's good? Yo, I'm about to drop y'all off. My brother said he don't feel like driving back across town."

Then he turned the car on and started backing the car out the driveway.

"Devon spoke out. What about Rhonda?"

"Oh, yeah. She said she good. She staying a bit longer."

Randy and Devon both looked at each other and felt a little odd. Then the guy driving said loudly :

" That smells like some kush y'all smoking on back there ."

"Let me hit that shit."

Randy took another puff of the blunt and passed it to the guy driving. He started smoking the blunt, coughed a bit and said:

"This is really some good smoke!" Then glanced back at Randy for a second and asked him:" Can I buy some of that smoke off you?"

He answered.

" Yea but I'm on my last 10."

The guy said:

" Cool. I'm going to stop at the corner store down the way so y'all can grab a swisher."

Devon spoke out.

""I'm straight. I ain't even trying to smoke for real. I'm just trying to get back to the crib so I can relax and get ready for school tomorrow." The driver again replied this time in a demanding voice.

"I'm gonna get y'all there. Don't worry." Randy looked at Devon and said:

" Let me sell him this weed real quick. This will be some easy cash!"

They drove down a couple blocks when they pulled up to a small bright lit up deli Market. the

The sky was now dark and stars were beginning to form and align. Randy handed the driver the bag of weed.

The driver sniffed the marijuana and said:

"It' sure! Smells good!" Then turned to Randy and asked him:

" How much?"

"Hold up. Let me run in the store and get change, I'll grab some Swisher's, you still matching me up right?" The guy nodded his head then Randy opened up his door and got out the car, then called to Devon:

" You coming in, fam?" Devon thought about it and was just about to say no when he realized that all this sitting around had made him thirsty.

He hopped out the car and yelled back to Randy:" here I come". As they entered the store Devon tapped Randy and said:

"You want something to drink? I'm about to get something".

Randy nodded and headed towards the front register.

" The drinks were at the back of the Store as." Devon opened each cooler to decide what he wanted- his eyes were caught by the beer. He thought about a 24 ounce can but grabbed a cream soda and Hawaiian Punch instead since he was on his way home.

Then he headed back to the front of the store. Once he got to the front, he was surprised to see Randy had got the swisher with no problem this time.

"How were you able to purchase those with no ID?"

"Shut up dude. The guy behind the counter was cool about it. He wasn't even tripping." After the boys got the two drinks, paid for they both prepared to leave the store.

Devon opened the door and was the first to step out into the now very cold air .What he saw nearly shocked him to death. He froze exactly where he stood. Randy bumped into him.

" Where the hell is the car?" He was in full disbelief.

The parking lot was empty. They were now stranded somewhere. They had no idea where . They didn't even know this area well. Randy then spoke out angrily:

"He got over on me! He didn't even pay for that weed I just sold him . Fuck! " Devon reacted with even more anger and intensity in his voice.

" Fuck that bum ass weed fucking with! You got me stranded out , here Randy!"

He looked back at him.

"Devon, who do you think you're talking to like that??"

He was just about to charge at Devon When they both turned, they heard a loud voice coming from a man.

"What y'all got in them pockets?" They heard him say.

The two boys both looked at each other and absolute terror. A group of six dudes came from the side of the store charging right for them. Devon tried to react but it was too late. One of the dudes hit him in the ribs with a metal pole. He screamed almost immediately. He felt the pain flowing through his body, crushed to the ground and started coughing loud and vigorously. He glanced up for a split moment to see Randy jerking and squirming- they were having a harder time with him. One of the taller guys pinned him against the building while two others continued to take hard straight punches to his face. Then Devon quickly felt the pain of being trampled on, he was getting stumped ragged while he was on the ground and he could feel his pockets being emptied. He slowly started drifting in and out of consciousness. He could hear Randy shouting "no get off me!" several times. He heard a very loud ear ringing gunshot. Had he been shot? Sirens filled up his ear as he totally blacked out into darkness

CHAPTER 2

Total darkness reappeared. A man alike some type of vigilante was shouting:

"You belong to us. Why would you think you could ever escape?"

There he was again, it was the same man from before, dressed all in black with the black cloak around his neck. Two other men were holding him by each arm. Another man walked up in front of him and with the same loud voice from before said :

"Yo, you're stupid. You cannot escape us. You're nothing but a sorry piece of trash. We own you. Remember that!"

He had an evil grin on his face. The man dressed in all black with the cloak looked terrified, he was being held against his will . Then he cried out:

"What have I done to deserve this?"

The other man yelled back at him.

"Shut your mouth" Then disrespectfully spit in his face.

The man that wore all black screamed in anger as the two men continue to grip both his arms tightly. The spit ran all the way down his face and onto his shirt. Now the other man spoke again, very loudly.

"Now take him out there!"

The two men grabbed the man with all black by his arms and started directing him somewhere as they walked and got close. They could hear thousands of people screaming and shouting.

The man in black instantly knew where he was going. The two men released him and shoved him forward. He didn't speak at all, the man in black turned one more time and walked from behind a curtain and pitted himself for what he was about to do he walked out onto a stage platform of some sorts with bright lights shining high above him.

The thousands of people got even louder, almost enraged. It seems like screaming turned into shouting. The spotlight was on him. He was all alone.

"Let me out! Let me out, my mind my soul! I have no control. Where am I? Who am I I'm lost, confused. Stuck in chaos!" Then he started chanting and saying the same words he spoke before:" cisum detavitom lla yad yadyreve I will die, but I vow he will return for revenge he will return and change what's been done."

The darkness comes again. A beeping noise starts repeating over and over.

"Devon wake up." Someone calls out. He blinks several times trying his hardest to regain consciousness.

" Devon! Wake up!" The voice calls again. He then opens his eyes to see his mother Nevaeh Gates Smith standing over him.

"Hey, baby, how are you? You scared us! "

Devon blinked again in pure delusion.

"Where am I? " He asked his mother. She looked down at him sternly. You could tell by the bags under her eyes and the roughness in her face that she hadn't slept much lately.

"You're in the city hospital. You`ve been beat up pretty bad. The doctors said you have dislocated your ribs and a partially broken arm. That should heal in a few weeks."

Devon looked up to his mom in shock.

"How did I get here? I don't remember too much. I just know that…." he paused. "Wait a minute. Me and Randy were at a corner store and then… hold up. Where is Randy?"

His mother turned away from him looking out the hospital window. When she turned back you could see she had a little tear in her eye.

" Your friend Randy… He he's dead." She answered. Shamefully, Devon almost choked on his own saliva. He couldn't breathe for a minute. He tried to pretend he didn't hear her right.

"What mom? he asked, she uttered back:

" Yes. You heard me right, your friend was shot last night. He didn't make it. They did everything they could."

There was a heavy silence in the room for a while. Devon eye's became very watery. Then he looked back at his mother and spoke.

" That could have been me. Mom, a group of guys jumped us and robbed us as well."

"I figured something like that happened. But the question that we all want to know is what were you doing all the way across town so far away from home? And I actually called you several times and you never called to let me know that you were okay. I was worried sick.. I called the school. I got a call at 2:00 in the morning that you were admitted into emergency and your friend was in intensive care."

" I'm sorry, mom. I messed up. I made a bad choice. I should have came home straight after school. "

"It's okay." Nevaeh replied. "We're not going to worry about that now, just focus on getting better. But when you get home best believe there will be some form of punishment."

" Okay. "

" I have to go back home and make sure your sister has something to eat for dinner. I'll be back first thing in the morning. I'm glad you're conscious and aware. You were knocked out for a full 24 hours."

He didn't answer but looked up to see the clock hanging on the wall. It read 8:30 p.m.

"They said that when they brought you here you were pretty much in and out of consciousness, calling out for your dad several times. I'm just extremely glad that my baby is okay. And when you're well we're going to make sure we're all at church on Sunday to thank the Lord for this. "

Devon nodded his head.

" How many more days will I have to be here?"

"Maybe a couple, they just have to run a few more tests to make sure everything's working properly. I'll see you in the morning."

She then leaned close to him and planted a loving kiss right on his forehead.

" I love you, son. "

"I love you, too."

After his mom left the hospital, he sat in bed and turned on the T.V, scrolling through the stations to find a channel where the NBA basketball game was. He tried to move his body to the edge of the hospital bed, but he could tell he was still so sore and weak. Feeling the urge to use the restroom, he noticed he was hooked up to some form of wire. So he couldn't move even if he wanted to. Once the nurse came back in his room she said hello and pleasantly smiled at him

"Good to see you're awake and active. You were out of it for a little while." He smirked.

"I'm glad I'm up and alert too. What is this tool? I'm hooked up to it. I can't even leave my bed. "

Oh, that's a catheter. We put that in you for when you were unconscious. It's in your bladder. So you can properly handle your business and remove fluids from your body. Now that you're active I will ask the doctor to remove it. Is there anything else you need?"

" No."

The nurse disappeared back into the hospital hallway. Devon started back watching the NBA game. He could feel he was getting a little drowsy and without noticing drifted back off into a comforting slumber. The next morning, Devon awoke to notice he was no longer tied to his hospital bed. He still yawned loudly and stretched his tender bones thinking: "I'm definitely feeling a lot better." He walked over to his hospital window. It was a cloudy, dreary morning. Rain was coming down from the light grey sky.

"I should probably call my mom to let her know I'm feeling a lot better."

As soon as he reached for the phone next to his bed, he suddenly heard a gentle knock at the hospital room door. A caramel skin, blond haired girl entered. At first, Devon didn't recognize her then it quickly came to him.

"Rhonda!! What are you doing here?"

"I just came to see if you are all right, I heard about your accident." She answered back quickly. "I just came to see if you were all right, I heard about your accident." Devon responded back in rage :

"Accident... That was no accident. We were set up then." He took his eyes off Rhonda, lowered his head and continued. "You probably heard that Randy's dead. He was shot that night and wasn't able to pull it through. Do you hear that? He's dead!"

His eyes glazed right into hers .

"Were you in on it? In on what?"

She screamed back.

"We were set up that night and you so happened to not be with us. "

She looked back surprised at Devon as if she was offended.

"No, I had no idea but we both know who really did."

" Yeah, I know exactly who. But why should I believe you? You`re just a ratchet chick I met in front of a corner store."

Rhonda screamed back even louder.

"Who are you talking to like that?"

He was just about to respond when the phone rang and broke the hostility in the room. He grabbed the phone on the third ring and said hello.

"Hey, son. Are you feeling better?" and Devon realized it was his father's voice.

"Hey, dad. Yes, I'm feeling a lot better. Actually, I'm glad you called to check on me."

" Of course." His dad said? "I love you. I'm just glad you're okay. Son, you gave me and the rest of the family quite a scare. "

Meanwhile the nurse slipped in the room and asked Rhonda to leave so the doctor could come in and speak with Devon.

" He just needs to sign the paperwork so he can leave today." The nurse whispered to Rhonda.

"We want to speak to you for a second so we can get you on out of here." She said with a smile on her face. Devon spoke back into the phone.

"They're going to release me today."

"That's what's up. I'll be up there, to pick you up. "

 Let me wrap this up here at the office and see you afterwards. "

Devin hung the phone up. He turned to face both the doctor and nurse, the doctor spoke sternly.

"Will release you today, but these next couple of days you will have to really take it easy, young man. I want you to understand that you're very blessed to make it out of this situation you were in, this could have been the end for you too. . So hold your head up and try to make better decisions, next time. From one black man to another black young man… You don't want to become another statistic. You hear me?"

 Devon stood up and shook the doctor's hand.

"Thank you!

"Your dad should be here soon. I'll have the nurse bring you your release papers. Take it easy. Okay?"

When the doctor exited the room, he sat down for a minute and thought about the conversation he had with Rhonda.

"I might have been a little hard on her, but I just don't know. All I know is my friend. Randy is gone and that could have easily been me instead."

Before he knew it, it was Sunday. The first couple of days, Devon was very quiet. He had barely said a word. On Sunday, he was a little more upbeat. He ate breakfast and prepared for church.

At church, the preacher spoke a sermon that went really well with what they had just gone through. It was about how we should cherish our lives and we should in every situation . They also had heavy prayer over his dead fallen friend Randall. Devon watched in amazement as his 12 year old sister Heaven Gates Smith sang a song in front of the entire church. She has such a wonderful voice and he was proud to watch his sister up there singing. After church, Devon, his sister and parents headed home and had a very pleasant surprise waiting for them: when they walked inside their house they were first greeted by the pleasant aroma of their favorite meal: fried chicken, Great Northern beans and honey cornbread.

" Hey family!" Afamiliar voice said from the TV room uncle Doug Devon shouted.

" When did you get here? "

"I wanted to surprise you. So how is everyone? How's my baby brother? " And reached for Devon's dad Daniel Gates

He wanted to playfully wrestle with him. Daniel ducked out of his brother's reach.

" We didn't tell the kids you were in town. We wanted them to be surprised. ".

"By the smell of that wonderful food,it seems like Sunday dinner is almost finished."

Heaven agreed.

"Dad it smells so good!"

"You guys ready to eat?"

 Aunt Cynthia yelled walking out of the kitchen chewing on a piece of fried chicken.

"Mmm. It's hot and ready !"

Everyone laughed and rushed to sit down. After the meal, everyone was happy and stuffed. Heaven, aunt Cynthia, Daniel and Nevaeh were all chilling, watching a movie and Devon was off letting Uncle Doug here his brand new hip-hop CD. That was the reason he was excited when his uncle came around, because Devon knew he used to work for a major record label and he had plenty of music industry resources that his uncle could use to help him get a record deal.

"Not bad, nephew you have got a lot better since the last time I heard you, but you still have room to grow."

"Uncle Doug, listen to another couple songs." Then Devon looked at him. "Can you give me a record deal, please? I'm ready. I'm really, really ready. I got the skills. You hear me."

His uncle laughed.

"Yeah you cool, but you need to first finish the senior year and walk that stage and then maybe we could talk."

Devon had a disappointed look on his face. He shook his head.

"Okay. Yeah, I will, don't worry."

Uncle Doug grabbed Devon by the shoulder then looked into his eyes.

"You have to promise me one more thing: you have to promise to never let anything happen to your sister. You hear me? Make sure you protect her with your life."

The sounds of thunder roared loudly through the dark lit sky. Heaven Gates Smith abruptly wakes up from a really horrible nightmare, drenched in sweat.

" That dream was harsh."She thought to herself. She could hear the rain showering down, hard against the roof of her home. Did she hear it again? Wait, was it a dream? She could hear her parents downstairs, screaming. She couldn't tell what they were arguing about, but she definitely knew that the intensity of their arguing was very frightening. Before she could make it out her bed to see what exactly was going on, she heard gunshots coming from somewhere in the house. She immediately hopped out of bed and darted down the hall to her brother Devon's room, only to find him not in his bed. Where is he? She nervously wondered then she spun around in fear as she heard sirens getting closer and closer to the house.

Heaven suddenly heard her brother Devon's voice downstairs yelling and crying.

"No, no. No, it can't be. What have I done?" She heard him say as she walked downstairs to see where all the commotion was coming from. She stood frozen. Devon was on his knees. His eyes were bulging out repeating those same words.

"No, no. No, he can't be what have I done?" Heaven yelled.

"What are you talking about? What have you done? And where's Mom and Dad? I heard them. I heard the gunshots." Devon didn't answer but there was blood everywhere. She was so scared. Then she heard these terrifying words coming from his mouth.

"Mom and dad are dead, Heaven. And it's all my fault."

Before Heaven could respond two paramedics arrived. A police officer came rushing through the door.

"Put your hands up where I can see them!" The officer yelled.

Heaven hadn't noticed before but she could now see her father's lifeless body over in front of his office door.

"Dad!!" She cried out. She ran over and saw her mom laying dead with bullet holes in her, on the floor between the door of the kitchen , Heaven cried out even louder. She stood over her mom where a 38 revolver was dropped next to the body.

She yelled:

" Oh my God. Who killed them?"

The officer shouted again.

" Put your hands in the air! No, as a matter of fact you're both under arrest!"

Heaven was too much in shock to hear what the policeman had actually said , her body she felt numb and she could barely breathe. The officer walked over to her and yelled one more time:

"Did you hear me? You're under arrest and so are you!" He pointed his pistol directly where Devon was.

"Slouched over on the floor!! Whose gun is that?" The officer demanded an answer. " I need more backup here" He voiced in his radio. "I don't know what happened here. You're both going with me."

" No, leave her out of it !" Devon shouted. "This is all my fault, believe me this is all my fault."

He repeated. You could see tears running down his face. The officer handcuffed and walked him out. Heaven was so confused and her mind was in total disarray. She wanted this to be a bad dream or even an extreme nightmare, but no, this was indeed her new reality.

Daniel Gates Smith drove up his driveway, got out of his car and walked through the grass towards the front door of his home. As he walked, he thought to himself how great of a family he had and how blessed he was. He was retired from the NFL, lived a very happy life with two children- a daughter and son, he also had such a beautiful wife. When he walked through the door, he could smell the sensational scent of cabbage cornbread and pork roast coming from the kitchen.

" Actually the aroma was covering the entire house, baby." He called out to his wife Nevaeh.

She came walking from the kitchen.

"Hey, honey! You hungry? I have your plate waiting for you. It was so good! Everyone else ate already , Heaven is up in her room getting ready for bed. I think Devon left to hang out with friends. Okay?"

"Hmm. I can't wait to taste some of that buttery corn bread. I'ma just warm my plate up and eat while I watch the Lakers game." He told his wife. She planted a juicy kiss on his lips.

"Okay. Let me just grab a couple of wine coolers from the basement and I'll join you." Daniel slapped Nevaeh on the ass, then walked over to the TV room with his plate. He turned on the 60-inch TV and started watching the game. Nevaeh joined him with two cups of wine and a small bottle of tequila. She smiled at her husband and said "now the party can really get started". He laughed and pulled her down right next to him on the couch. They watched the game, laughed, talked and even fore-played a bit. The game ended at about 1:15 a.m. Both Daniel and Nevaeh were a bit tipsy from the bottle of tequila. They started kissing each other very vigorously and Daniel started to take his pants off. He was prepared to make love to his wife when he was interrupted by some noise coming from the front door. It opened and he could hear the sounds of voices walking into the house. He shushed Nevaeh so he can listen to what was happening in the other room. He could clearly hear his son. Devon was having a very serious conversation with a teenage girl.

"Wait, I can't go through with this. I have to make sure my parents are not home first. My mom told me at dinner that she was going to meet my dad at the casino and they won't be back until early in the morning."

Daniel heard this and turned to his wife whispered:

"Something is going down in there. I'm not sure but we're going to keep quiet, like we're not here." Nevaeh attested.

" Why would we do that? It`s a childish idea!" A moment later. Devon called out to them.

"Dad, are you home? Are you awake?" Then heard him say to the girl: "everyone's asleep if they are here. My sister's upstairs in her room. So let's make this quick. Let's hurry and get this over with. Tell them we will be out shortly."

But before he could finish two teenage boys came bursting through the door.

" How much longer is this going to take?"

" Actually we will help you speed things up."

" Your dad has plenty of luxuries you can hand over to help you pay off what you owe and square your debt."

Devon looked at one of the taller boys and with a very angry expression on his face.

" Look, you all need to chill. I agree to swipe some cash to pay off the drug money I lost but I didn't need everybody here on my neck while I'm trying to do this. I'm not even sure when my parents will be back. "

"So we need to hurry this up."

"Y'all better get the fuck out of my house right now!"

" Or what ?" The other boy cut Devon off. "We own you." He shouted." You work for our boss" and showed him a 38 revolver tucked between his pants. "I don't want to have to use this." He looked up at Devon with a smirk on his face.

Devon ignored him, turned away and stepped in his dad's office.

He quickly started searching the room for any valuables. The two boys and the girl walked in the room behind Devon, one of the boys called to him.

"Hey some of those NFL trophies might work." He pointed over to a shelf that had several of Devon's dads NFL trophies lined up on it.

"No, I can't touch any of those. My Dad will notice they are missing."

 "Well, we don't care what you say. We will grab anything as long as it's worth the money you owe. "

The boy started to say something else but stopped when he noticed a large-sized metal safe in the far corner of the room. He turned and looked at his two other accomplices to see if they had seen what he did and they did. He loudly called out to Devon.

"Look over there! Open that treasury! I'm not asking! I'm telling you!"

Then he pulled out the 38 revolver and aimed it right at Devon's head who instantly stopped moving. They hesitated.

"Man, what are you doing? " He shouted

"Did you hear what I said?"

"Yeah. I heard you." Devon answered." But I'm not sure I know or remember the pass code".

"Well, you better remember it right now or we're going to have a problem here."

Meanwhile, down the hall, in the TV room Nevaeh and her husband were trying to listen closely to the altercation. But now it was very hard to hear what the kids were saying since they were down in another room.

"Wait, baby. I think they're in my private office." Daniel told Nevaeh. "I thought I'd locked the door, but it definitely sounds like they're down there now and having some kind of argument. Let's hurry down there. "

"Stop. Whatever it is that's going on, I don't like it and Devon shouldn't even have those kids in our home and especially in your private office. What do you think he's doing?" She asked her husband.

"I`m not sure hon. He is probably showing off my spectacular trophies and awards." Daniel said sarcastically then looked at his wife with a smile.

"It's not funny." Nevaeh responded in a very serious voice. "Like I said, I really, really don't like this. Something just doesn't feel right, baby."

"All right, let's sneak out the side door and come back through the front like we were never here. Then we will crash their little party and they'll be so shocked to see us and never know that we were here the whole time. Besides, how much harm could they do? It's just a bunch of teenagers."

He looked at his wife as he reached to reassure her. They quietly left out the house prepared to sneak back in. They had no idea they were about to find out just how dangerous teenagers really can be.

"Man, I said hurry! "The taller boy yelled at Devon. "We just know that the safe has money in it."

The girl said:

"Sweet, this will be even better. We won't have to hit any pawn shops or sell anything. Will have cash right in our hand."

Devon started using the combination to open the safe. "Why would I ever bring strangers into my home and think everything will go accordingly? How stupid of me but too late now. This is actually happening." The girl spoke up again.

"Sorry to do this to you dude but you're late on your payments and you know how our boss can be. We'll get our cut just for taking care of the business. So that's exactly what we're doing. "

" I'm not sorry." The other boy laughed. I definitely need this extra money. So let's see what we're working with."

He finished the last number of the combination then slowly opened the safe. His mouth dropped . It seemed like there were four or five hundred thousand dollars laying in the safe. Before anyone could say a word Devon's dad. Daniel yelled into the room.

"What y'all doing here?" He said in a very loud, angry voice that startled the kids so much that the boy with the revolver turned so fast, and he without noticing fired the 38 right into Mr. Smith's leg.

"Oh, wow."

He screamed in agony as the bullet shot through his left lower leg. He fell to the ground immediately. The teenagers shouted out and sheer horror. No one could believe what just happened . Daniel laid on the floor crying in pain. Nevaeh rushed into the room and broke the awed silence. She screamed in terror.

"What have you done? "

She looked around the room then spotted Devon. She yelled :

"Quick grab something to tie his leg with or he will bleed out !Who did this?"

She asked the boy holding the gun.

"You weren't supposed to be here. At least, that's what he told us. Didn't mean to shoot him but we are taking all this money and your son owes to some important people. We came to collect his debt."

 Nevaeh yelled back at the boy.

"No, you're not taking shit. And you know what? I'm calling the police."

Then darted from the room to go grab her cell phone. The boy aimed the gun to stop Nevaeh and his two accomplices ran out the room after her.

Devon screamed.

"Don't touch my mom. "

He tried to follow but before he could react, the boy with the revolver hit Devon in the back of the head with it. Devon fell to the ground and passed out from the blow he just suffered. The boy then turned his attention back to Devon's dad who was also still laying on the floor, breathing very slowly with a puddle of blood up under him.

" Damn this has really turned ugly." He thought to himself. "We got to find a way out of this situation."

Then the sounds of screams and glass shattering down the hall in the kitchen startled him. He hurried to find out what exactly was going on. As he stormed into the kitchen, he could see Nevaeh shouting: "stay away from me" while waving a butcher knife gripped firmly in her right hand. His two accomplices were trying their best to control her to no avail. The teenage girl yelled:

"Fuck , she just cut me!"

Nevaeh reached for her cell phone on the kitchen counter. The blast of the gun shot out two more times it rang again throughout the house. Everything seemed to go in slow motion . Nevaeh collapsed to her knees. She had been shot clear in her chest and another time just above her neck blood was gushing out everywhere. The teenage girl turned.

"Why did you shoot her? "

You could hear the fear and agitation in her voice.

" Shut up before I shoot you too! "

The girl immediately went quiet. To her disapproval the other teenage boy spoke up.

" That lady was about to call the police, but you didn't have to shoot her. We had it under control. Now she is laying dead and we have more of a mess to clean up."

The boy with the gun smirked, aiming the revolver right at his face and spoke those same words.

"Shut up or I will shoot you, I'm running the show here. Now go bag up the rest of the money so we can finish this and get out of here the two followed his orders. and Started loading the money in the bags!"

They each filled up their own separate bag. The boy with the revolver laughed out loud.

" There is enough here for us all to get the pay cut we rightfully deserve. There's only one last thing to do."

 As he spoke those next few words with a horrifying expression defined on his face.

"No witnesses! No fucking loose ends! "

He walked out the office door right in front of where Mr. Smith had crawled and now was laid sprawled out barely moving.. He looked him right in the eyes and shot a bullet directly through his skull execution style. The girl yelled: "fuck this" grabbed the bag of money, darted out the room to the hall towards the front door.

 The boy with the gun screamed:

"Stop right now!" Aiming the firearm at the running girl as if he was prepared to shoot it off again, but his a male accomplice grabbed him from behind and tried to get the gun away from him. They wrestled and tussled for a couple of minutes. Shocked and confused, Devon woke back up and watched the two boys punching away at each other and realized the gun was laying on the ground near the scuffle. He immediately rushed to pick it up and grabbed it, then shot towards the two boys yelling "get the fuck out of my house right now before I kill you." Neither of the boys hesitated. Both of them got to their feet and ran as fast as they could out the front door, never looking back.

Devon collapsed because his head was pounding. He was delirious and felt like he had a concussion. He couldn't believe how horrible this night had turned. He felt the blood gushing out of his head down the back of his neck. He stumbled around trying to gather his footing then he noticed his father laying on the floor with a wicked bullet hole directly through his head. Tears started flowing down Devon's face.

"No, no, no!" He cried to himself while staring at his dad's lifeless body. He hadn't even noticed that he still was gripping the gun that caused his night to turn for the worst. When he discovered his mother was laying in front of the kitchen door with multiple bullet holes in her , Devon screamed:

" Mom."

He squeezed the handle of the firearm with anger and rage.

" Those fuckers will pay for this. But, this is all my fault. "

He stood Frozen in place as he could hear police and ambulance sirens getting closer and closer. He could hear his sister Heaven calling his name from upstairs. He ignored her calls he squeezed his dad's now dead body

"Dad. Wake up. Please dad. Wake up. "

He heard the sirens even closer now probably on his street, then he totally blacked out and couldn't hear anything, but he could clearly see his sister Heaven screaming at the top of the stairs , having a panic attack upon seeing the devastation. She came downstairs to witness.

CHAPTER 3

After a dreadful long week Heaven decides not to return to school and plans to leave the city for good. She desperately wants to forget about what happened the night her parents died. She feels so hurt and confused, empty like she is left alone in the world. Her best friend Tiffany tries to help and motivate her. She wants Heaven to change her mind about wanting to leave the city. She offers her a way to make some quick cash by telling her about a group of Friends planning to invade a local Pawn shop for some valuables and how they could make $5,000 dollars a piece, if they did the job successfully. Heaven seriously considers her friend Tiffany's offer because she doesn't have any of her own money right now or even a clear plan or direction on what to do next. Due to some legal complications and the severity of the crime all of her parents finances and assets were frozen. Later that day Heaven called her Uncle Doug. He tells her he would help with the funeral arrangements and also offers her a place to stay if she wants to come live with him and his wife, Cynthia in Virginia. She tells him she's not sure maybe she will decide after the funeral.

Heaven Gates Smith woke up on this rainy, dark, dreary morning. She let out a big sigh to herself as she rolled over out off the bed, She had a bad feeling like a big knot in her stomach. When she looked out, the light rain was drizzling outside her window. She then looked over to the small vanity mirror that she had across from her bed and said to herself:" Well, mom and dad, today's the day. I finally get to lay you to rest." Looking up towards the sky she shouted: "Lord. Give me all the strength. I need to get through today." Having said that out loud , she sat on the edge of her bed about to get up and head to the bathroom to shower and get ready for her parents, Nevaeh and Daniel Gates Smith`s funeral. Yes, today was the day. Even though Heaven had been preparing herself for this day all week, she still felt lost, hurt and overwhelmed. Due to her anxiety , she was an emotional wreck this morning. Days like these were the ones in which Heaven would usually call her mom to help get her anxiety back down. She thought about it as she turned on the shower and adjusted the water as hot as she could make it. Heaven then went back into the room with her mind racing super fast, trying to think of everything. She still had to prepare for her parents funeral. Heaven was really rushing around like a chicken with its head cut off. With the unfolding anxiety, she was overwhelming herself for sure. She then took three big breaths as a form of motivation- she learned that from her counselor she had in Middle School. This breathing exercise would usually work for heaven but not today, which was probably because Heaven was about to see both of her parents in their coffins. They would be sitting side-by-side in colored caskets: one pink powder pink - her mother's favorite color, and a soft, almost powder blue- which was Daniel Gates Smith's favorite color.

Heaven, then opened up her drawer to take out her black, lace Fendi dress. It was one of her favorite designers. She had her outfit hanging up on a hanger, in front of her closet door. She then laid her dress on the bed, turning around to get her black lace stockings from her top panties drawer, which she also laid out on her bed. Heaven then put her hand up to her forehead to check and see if her temperature was going up or if she was getting hot. She couldn't decide which shoes she was going to wear today. Heaven leaned over to her small wooden antique alarm clock to see what time it was. She had got it from her grandmother for her 13th birthday. The time was 7:35 am in the morning.

"Let me hurry up and stop procrastinating." Heaven said to herself.

The funeral was going to start at 12, which were the calling hours for the service and the viewing was from 10 a.m. The funeral home had told the family to arrive early to make sure all the details were. in order. They would also do the first and final viewing of her parents bodies before the actual funeral service would start. So as Heaven took another three deep breaths to regroup and calm down, her thoughts , anxiety and emotions kept steady pace. She wanted to be as calm as she could be before she arrived at the church. She planned to get there early so she could make sure her parents final details were all in order for the final farewell, which is the hardest thing to do. It was going to be a very emotional, sad and overwhelming day.

Heaven then rushed in the bathroom and jumped in the shower that she had left the running water for 30 minutes now. The water was steaming hot. Heaven looked at her phone again before getting in the shower, the time on her phone said 8:30 a.m. "Oh boy time always fly when you have something important to do." She said to herself. Heaven then quickly showered and brushed her teeth, it only took her about 10 to15 minutes to get done. She was moving at a fast pace so that she can make it to the church on time. Luckily, the funeral place was only 5 to 10 minutes away. Heaven started to pull up her stockings. She had just got finished putting on her mother's favorite lotion- Coco by Chanel 5. She then put on three to four squirts of the matching Coco Chanel perfume. Heaven then put on her black lace dress and her mother's favorite dress shoes, which were made by another famous designer- they were black suede Michael Khors heels with off-white little pearls that wrapped around the straps with a small 3 inch heel.

She remembered those were the shoes her parents had got her for her 11th grade formal school dance. Heaven started to cry. She knew that she was never going to see her parents again after today. Heaven was ready and dressed now. As she was on her way out the door, she took one last look at herself in the mirror - her mascara was starting to run down her face from her tears. She then quickly grabbed a few tissues to wipe it before she headed out .

It was now ten minutes till 9:00. Heaven was supposed to be at the church by 9 a.m. Luckily, it was only a five minute drive from the house. Heaven had been so emotional and overwhelmed that she had forgotten she told her best friend Tiffany that she would ride with her to the funeral. After all, Tiffany knew that Heaven would be in no state of mind to be driving by herself . Heaven opened the front door , Tiffany was already parked in front of the house waiting for her to come out. Heaven looked up and headed to the car. She told Tiffany:

" Girl., I'm so freaking emotional and physically drained already."

"I'm here for you girl and I will be here every step of the way. "

"Thank you so much !"

Heaven said as the two girls pulled off and headed to the church Heaven and Tiffany arrived at the church. They both let out a big "wow" at the same time. They both saw how many cars were already there and it was just now about to be the calling hours. They looked at each other, locked eyes for a few seconds got out of the car and headed to the church . Heaven still had a big knot in her stomach. She was trying not to break down yet. She was trying to stay strong. The girls got closer to the church front door when they both saw a small black cargo van pulled out from the church's back driveway. The van had "County Sheriff's Office" on the side of it in yellow writing. Heaven then saw a boy waving bye to her through the van`s window. That's when she noticed. It was her brother. It was Devon. She said to Tiffany.

"Wow, I didn't even know they would let him attend. Attend today With him being charged with the murder. Hmm. "

"Yeah, that's crazy." Said Tiffany to her best friend. "Well, I guess you're considered innocent until proven guilty and they are his parents too. "

"Anyway, I don't want to believe my brother would have committed the murders. I just can't right now." said Heaven." I have a funeral to think about right now."

"Yes you`re right." said Tiffany. "Let's get in there. We got this!"

Heaven got inside. The lady from the funeral home was waiting . She greeted her, giving her deepest condolences.

"You're right on time. We wanted you to make sure both of your parents are presentable and up to your standards."

" Okay."

They walked in, having seen her parents laying in their caskets side by side, she told the funeral home they did a great job with her mother and father . She looked at both her parents -they laid there in the caskets looking almost if they were sleeping. Heaven checked out her mom first : she looked like a sleeping angel in her soft pink casket. She was wearing a white Givenchy designer dress that Heaven had picked out for her . It was also the one her mother wore for her 20th year marriage anniversary, which was exactly three weeks before the murders happened. Heaven just smiled as Tears began to fall. She then turned to Tiffany and told her she did a great job on her mother's hair and makeup.

"Oh ,Tiffany. You know just how my mom did her makeup- not too much just enough. "

"Yes, girl."

" You nailed it."

Heaven looked at her mom again. She wore her favorite shade of lipstick, which was a soft burnt orange..

"She looks just like an angel laying there in her white dress." said Heaven.

Then turned to her father kissing him on the cheek saying "this is it Daddy no more pain. You and mom can rest now." Her father was also wearing all white, matching his wife. Nevaeh Daniel was wearing the white Balenciaga suit that he wore on the couple's 20th anniversary . Heaven also put on her daddy's gold Marc Jacobs watch that both her and Devon got him for his 45th birthday last year.

 Heaven then sat down in front of both her parents as she saw her friends , family and co-workers of her parents coming over to see the two fallen angels for the last time., Each time they would hug Heaven afterwards, telling her how sorry they were for her and Devon's loss and that if she needs anything at all to not be afraid to ask. But Heaven just sat there filled with so much pain. Everything people were saying went through one ear and out the other. She was feeling so empty and numb. She couldn't believe she was really burying not one parent, but both of them. Heaven began to rock back and forth back as tears started rolling and couldn't stop. She sat in the church trying to cope with the fact that she was saying her last goodbyes to both her mother and her father. When the funeral came to an end, she stood up and she headed to the small hall room that the church had given her for the family repast. This is where they could eat dinner and have drinks to grieve and celebrate the lives of her parents . A lot of their friends and family members begin to fill the small room quite quickly.

 Heaven was sitting down at one of the small dinner tables that was being used for all the funeral guests. She had began talking to her uncle Doug who was from Virginia. He was actually suggesting to Heaven that she should come back to Virginia with him and his wife to live for a while. He also told Heaven that he doesn't think she should be alone here without any family around. She didn't really know what she wanted to do. So she told her uncle that she would think about it and let him know once the repast was over and all the guests were gone home. Shortly after having the talk with her uncle, she heard a loud noise from across the room. It was people shouting tables getting pushed over kids crying. It was just awful. Heaven couldn't believe the sounds. She rushed across the room to see what all the fuss and commotion was about .Once she got there she noticed a familiar face that she hadn't seen in a while.

"Alex! She shouted at the boy she knew what's going on. She asked out loud: "I can't believe that you guys are fighting at my parents ceremony." She then began to cry again. She was already having a hard time burying both her parents. Heaven then shouted in a high raspy voice.

"This is so freaking disrespectful. I can't believe my eyes. My parents were good people, they never in a million years would have disrespected anyone's home going day. Alex, I haven't seen you in almost two years after you and your family moved to New Jersey now you show up to my parent's home going fighting with my cousin ?"

Heaven then looked at her cousin then back to Alex with a disappointed, upset look on her face.

" I don't understand . What's the problem? Why are you two fighting anyways? What happened? Why today of all days?"

She was super close to Alex when they were kids . He also used to be

Best friends with both her and Tiffany until he and his family left town one day, moving to New Jersey without even saying goodbye. This left her with hurt feelings towards him for doing so. Alex began to apologize to Heaven for leaving in such a disappointing way. He then tried to apologize to Heaven's cousin, but her cousin just grabbed his jacket and left storming out in such an immature manner. Heaven just shook her head and gave Alex a chance to explain himself and his actions.

"Heaven first off, I'm so sorry for your loss. I caught the first plane out when I got the news. And also, I'm sorry I left without telling you goodbye .That was such a stupid thing for me to do to my friend of 10 plus years. I was just so angry at the time that I had to leave all my friends, my school, my hometown. And most of all, I'm so sorry for showing up acting like a complete idiot, fighting with your cousin. It's just that I saw Mike (who was a boy they both knew from middle school) and he was telling me that this whole time your cousin knew exactly who killed your parents. He's being so selfish and not telling anybody or getting involved. Because he's scared to get put in the middle of it all."

Heaven's mouth dropped as she listened to the words coming from Alex's mouth . He hugged Heaven with such a tight hug that she started crying again.

"That's your family, your blood ,cousin! And if he knows something about the murders, then he needs to say something, at least to you. I'm so sorry again for my actions ".

" It's okay. I totally agree and I accept your apology. Thanks for showing up and giving me your condolences. I know it's been awhile. But hey, let's just let the past be the past. "

"I agree." said Alex .

Heaven then walked outside with a concerned look on her face to get some air.

"Are you okay?" A family member asked her.

"Yes I just want to be alone for a second and get some fresh air . I'll be right back in a minute. "

 Left alone, she's going crazy ,pacing back and forth thinking to herself "why would my cousin keep such important information from me ? Why Lord? Why? heaven thought to herself?" The repast time was coming to an end. Heaven said her goodbyes to everyone but it was one thing on her mind and that she was determined to find out : her cousin had some explaining to do.

" I don't know what yet but I promise you, mom and dad. If it's the last thing I do, I will find out, I promise I will."

 She walked away determined to get to the bottom of the mysterious information she had heard today. Very emotional and confused, Heaven just wanted to get a clear understanding of what had taken place on this sad, dreary, long day.

After all the funeral drama Heaven was still considering taking up her uncle Doug's offer to leave L.A and move with him in Virginia.

 Due to all the stress of losing her parents, she immediately dropped out of school, even though it was her senior year with only five months left to graduate. Heaven started focusing all her time on making money. A couple of her friends set up a robbery for them to break into a local pawn shop. They were supposed to get five thousand dollars a piece, but with Heaven`s recent bad luck, her and the group of people that joined her were caught red handed during the robbery in the shop. A neighbor had spotted them going through a back window and called the police on them before they broke into the shop. Heaven was extremely nervous. Her stomach was in knots and she had to pee very, very badly. They filled up duffel bags with all kinds of jewelry, valuables and electronics. By the time they got to the cash register she could barely sit still.

She had to use the restroom really bad now and could barely hold it in any longer but there was no time. She stayed focused and started filling up her bag with money. She was just about to zip up her bag and head for the door when a group of policemen charged in the pawnshop. The armed guns and pointed directly at Heaven gave her a shock. All she could do is stand there frozen in place, urinating all over herself. She had never been so embarrassed in her life. She was charged with breaking and entering a private property and it landed her six months probation with GPS monitoring. And only because this was the first time she was ever in any serious trouble and the judge understood she just went through a heavy trauma with her parents being killed. He took it easy on her but with her now stuck on a GPS monitor probation program, Heaven began to get really depressed. She felt as if she has lost everything that was ever important to her. She just couldn't believe her parents were dead from gun violence, and her brother is facing a life sentence for the crime. Maybe even the death penalty. She shook those horrible thoughts from her head.

"I know my brother's innocent. He could never do something like this. "

She really wished. It was all a bad dream, but it was very all real. Her brother Devon was the only family member left in this world. She thought she could trust him but the situation had left Heaven in a really vulnerable state of mind . She tried to lay down and get some rest because the next day she had an appointment with her probation officer. She woke up early to catch the bus and while she was standing at the bus stop. She met a guy who was sitting on the bench and he kept staring at her . Then he finally said:

" Hey, what's your name? "

She tried to ignore him the first time but he asked the question again even louder this time.

"Hey you what's your name? "

Having turned to face him, Heaven answered, very shy and subtle.

"Hey, I'm Heaven and right now I'm not in the mood to talk."

The guy laughed with arrogance.

"Maybe I can help you with your situation. I see that GPS ankle monitor you have on. I can get it off for you."

"Can you?"

"Sure, my uncle has a car garage with the tools and equipment to get it off. I'm only sitting here at this bus stop so I can sell the rest of my nose candy. Wait right here. I parked down the street. I'll pull back up then we can head over there to set it up. You seem like a nice girl so I really want to help you out."

Heaven thought to herself:" I'm not sure if I can trust this guy, but I really want this monitor off my ankle."

The guy pulled back up and yelled:

" Get in so we can get a move on. Oh, yeah. My name is Jimmy, by the way, but everybody just calls me J-Roc."

 She rolled her eyes at him. Then hopped in her new found friend`s truck. She noticed he had a bunch of furniture and other scraping in the back of the truck including a bed. She gave him a confused look.

"This is how I make my money by hitting licks and scrapping junk and selling stuff."

 Heaven laughed at that thought and told him how she got into her current situation by trying to steal from the pawn shop.

"Well, y'all didn't have the coldest man on the job with y'all. That's why you got caught." He looked at her with a bit of an arrogant smile. She rolled her eyes again and turned the music up.

"This is my song." She yells. They rolled through the city bumping music. He turns to Heaven:

" Here, light this up!" and hands her a rolled marijuana joint. She looks at it a couple times before shaking her head:

"No. I don't smoke."

He smirks.

" Like chill, is only a little bit of Mary Jane. "

"Okay. I'll try it out. But when are we going to do what you said? I need to make sure this GPS monitor doesn't go off anytime time soon. "

" I'm going to take you to my uncle's garage in a bit. For now., we're going to get blazed, but when I get the monitor off for you, promise me you`ll roll to the club tonight with me for my homie`s mixtape release party. I need a date."

Heaven didn't really want to do it or go to a club but she agreed anyway. After about three or four hours of pointless riding around, meeting all J-Rocs friends and affiliates that he was showing off , Heaven was not impressed at all. But after smoking her first ever couple of blunts she was so high out of her mind that she couldn't even say too much. It was her first time smoking weed. So her brain was moving constantly. They walked to the beach and grabbed some ice cream.

They finally headed to his uncle's body shop. After they left his uncle's garage J-Roc drove Heaven back home, looked at her and said : "a promise is a promise."

"Okay."

" I'll be here to grab you at about 10.30pm so we'll be able to get your monitor off right before. 11:00 p.m. "

That was the GPS monitor Curfew. She agreed then got out the truck. He sped off bumping his music . Heaven thought to herself:" What have I got myself into?" She was so exhausted. She went right to her friend`s Tiffany guest bedroom and plopped down on her pillow. She had been staying with her since after the funeral . She remembered her brother`s big court date was coming up in a few weeks- this was the trial for the murder of her parents. The thought of it made her anxiety go up. Heaven was laying on her bed when Tiffany popped her head in the room.

" Hey girl! You ok ? Heaven, I was so worried about you ."

"I'm fine".

She then told Tiffany about her long day and shared with her how she had to go to the club tonight with the guy J-roc Heaven begged Tiffany to go with her and said "please I really need someone. I Trust with me."

"we'll have to sneak out. My mom will kill us if she finds out. She told me that you can't make

more mistakes or get in any more trouble while living here. She feels bad for your situation with your family and what happened to your parents and brother, but don't want me caught up in any trouble. But because I love you I'm down to go tonight. And I don't want to leave you hanging."

Then gave Heaven a big hug. When 10 p.m came around, Heaven was extremely nervous. She really didn't want to get in any more trouble. But what could she do? Peer pressure can be very tough. She was now coming down from the high created from the blunts she smoked earlier. She was so stoned. She finished putting her slutty ensemble together, underneath her pajamas. She wanted to impress J-roc so she was wearing some skimpy shorts and a very sexy top. She popped into Tiffany's room.

"We`re in luck, my mom said she was leaving tonight. So usually that means she won't be back till late, late. She won't have any idea we're gone."

Her mom yelled up stairs.

"I'm leaving out. I'll see you girls in the morning."

J-Roc didn't pull up until about 10:50 p.m. And he pulled up as usual with his music blasting . Heaven heard him outside and yelled out:

" Thanks for waking up the neighborhood. We're supposed to be sneaking out."

J-Roc told her to chill. It was so easy to get that monitor off her ankle. It only took a couple minutes.

"Now. Tell your friend to come on, we're about to start sipping good." He pulled out a whole gallon of Hennessy from the back seat and asked her:

" You drink liquor, right?"

"No, I really don't drink ". J-Roc looked at her and laughed .

" Well today girl you about to get drunk."

Tiffany hopped in the car and joined them and then they all headed to the club. J-Roc couldn't stop talking about how great of an artist his homie was. They were already headed to his release party but Tiffany and Heaven thought otherwise about his music. When they pulled up to the club, the line was kind of long. This was actually a very popular club . Heaven was really nervous. She really wasn't the going and out type. But by now the whole gallon of Hennessy was nearly empty. Tiffany was kind of drunk too, talking loud to J-roc as they walked to the entrance. They skipped past the entire line, she heard J-Roc tell the bouncer they were on the list as they walked in. It was crowded and jumping with so much excitement. Heaven took a step back thinking she saw someone. That made her feel instantly scared. She ignored the feeling and followed J-Roc and Tiffany to the stage. Everybody was dancing and moving , having a good time. Heaven felt so out of place.

" I want to introduce you to my homie." J-roc said "But I want you as turned up as everybody in here, I want you to pop one of these."

He reached in his pocket, then handed her an Oxycodone pill.

"What am I supposed to do with this ? "

"Go ahead take it! It's going to have you ready to have some fun."

With no worries, Heaven turned to Tiffany and she tells her to break it in half so she could have a piece of the Oxycodone pill too.

" I sneak in and take some of my mom's all the time."Tiffany confessed. Heaven broke the pill in half and followed Tiffany to the bar for tequila. They took a shot together. Soon enough, the liquor and the pill mix set in .Heaven felt like the club started spinning and she could barely find her balance .

A couple of guys tried to feel on her body but she shoved them in disgust and kept moving through the crowd of people.

"Where is the restroom?" She thought. Then she heard the music stop and someone grabbing the mic on stage. She assumed it was J-Roc`s music homie, but she didn't stop to check and see. She continued to look for the restroom. She walked in and ran some cold water out the faucet, then splashed it on her face.

It helped a little. She heard someone else was in one of the restroom stalls but she was too dizzy to look up and see who it was. Heaven was so drunk. She could barely stand.. Tiffany came through the restroom doors and shouted to her:

"Are you okay, girl?"

" No. I'm pretty messed up. I'm ready to go right now."

After she said that a caramel skinned, blonde dyed hair girl that was kinda chunky, as if she was maybe pregnant jumped out the restroom stall and screamed at Heaven.

"You're not going anywhere until we have a little talk. I know you. You're Heaven Gates Smith . Me and you brother Devon were really close."

She had a sadistic smile on her face and she pointed at her on stomach like she was hinting at something. My new boyfriend told me about what he and his homies did to your parents and your brother will go down for it. He will take the fall for the crime. And if you know, what's good for you, you will keep your mouth shut."

Then she charged towards Heaven with a pocket knife.

"Don't say a word about what you think or we will find you and kill you !"

Tiffany shouted "leave her alone" and charged towards to girl before she could get to Heaven.

 Heaven watched her friend grab the girl and she started having a feeling that she had not ever felt before- a feeling of pure anger and rage. Everything went black and she could hear three or four gunshots ringing close nearby.

CHAPTER 4

Heather woke up in so much fear. She had no idea where she was. She heard a deep voice and it made her open her eyes.

"You're going to be okay." It was the doctor standing over her." You seem to have had a wild night. "

"What happened?"

"Not too sure. You'll have to ask your friend in the next room. She is recovering well from a stab wound."

Heaven was so startled by the doctor's words. It almost made her pass back out.

"Wait. I cannot remember anything from last night. I totally blacked out. but I really do hope Tiffany is okay." Before she could finish her sentence, a familiar face walked into her hospital room. It was J-roc. She gave him a very mean stare. He asked:

" What is your problem Heaven? I'm so glad you're okay."

"Well first off, where were you last night when all this was happening? Did you know Tiffany was stabbed? I asked you where the fuck were you J-roc

"There was a shooting inside the club last night. Five people got shot and two of them even died. We had to get out of there. We had drugs on us and stuff and I really thought you and Tiffany left me. Believe me. Heaven, I would have never just left you like that."

"Whatever we just need to go check on Tiffany to make sure she's okay. The doctor says she's recovering over in the next room, so let's go see for ourselves."

"Okay."

J-Roc gave her a hug.

"How are you feeling though?"

"I'll be okay, a couple scuffs and scrapes, and when I blacked out I think I bumped my head but I must be in much better shape than Tiffany."

They started walking to her room. When they got to her room, she was awake but she told Heaven she was in a lot of pain due to getting stabbed in the abdomen. Luckily , the knife missed any major organs or arteries. Heaven gave her a big hug.

"I'm so glad you're okay. I really can't remember anything that happened last night, it's all a blur ."

J-roc also gave Tiffany a hug.

"I had no idea you two were still in the club. I thought you left me behind, it got wild so fast." Tiffany told them she came in the bathroom during the altercation with heaven and some girls. And when she stepped in to help she was stabbed and then heaven went crazy and started punching the girl. After that everything went black . Everybody in a room took a pause. It was really quiet for like two minutes. Heaven has a sad look on her face. She felt that Tiffany`s stabbing was all her fault. But her best friend is a trooper and a very positive person so she told Heaven:

"This isn't your fault. I'm okay. And if it happened again, I'll do it all over for you."

 Heaven shrugs with a sigh.

"Okay, girl. I`m so glad you're okay. "

"Yeah, the doctors say I can go home in a couple of days."

 Heaven was released later that day, but she promised to come back to check on her. J-Roc then asked Heaven if she needs a ride. She looked unsure but still answered with a "yeah". J-Roc grabbed her hand and said:

" Come on. I got you. I'm not going to let anything else happen to you, baby."

 Heaven actually felt kind of safe next to J-Roc with all that has happened in her life. So as they left the hospital J-Roc asked Heaven if she wanted to stay with him for a few days just until Tiffany was back home and everything died down. She agreed. J-Roc told her he had to make a few stops before they headed home.

He asked Heaven if she was cool with that or if she wanted him to run her to his spot first.

"I'm fine. I'll ride with you. I don't want to be alone right now."

" I won't be that long. I got you. "

They pulled up to a house that had a lot of guys sitting outside. He looked around and told Heaven he would be right back, then he grabbed a small, black Gucci bag out the back seat. It was clear to Heaven. He must have been making some kind of drug run of sort, but at the time she didn't care. She felt safe with him. She saw one of the guys take the black bag into the house. Five minutes later, he came back out and gave the bag back to J-roc.

He got back into the truck, opened the bag, pulled out some money, counted and put it in his pocket tossing the bag in the back seat.

"Do you want something to eat?"

"Sure."

They headed to a Chick-fil-A restaurant to get some food. Heaven had a gut feeling that she was dealing with a bad boy. She knew the type and if her parents were still alive, they wouldn't approve but she was still finding herself. After all the adversity she had been through , she was catching feelings for him. He was definitely a different type of guy than what she was used to. Even though she probably should have listened to her better judgment, Heaven didn't care. She knew he was a street boy. But he also had a kind heart and treated her good all the time. So she gave him a chance and each day they spent together, her feelings for him grew stronger and stronger. J-roc also had feelings for her. He told her:

"You're the perfect girl for me. I've been waiting for you all my life. You're different from any other girl I've dealt with. You're my little angel and I will forever protect you."

That made heaven open up to J-roc about what happened to her parents and her brother. She also told him that she knew who had really killed her parents and they had threatened her and told her if she said anything she was next. She got really emotional telling J-roc what happened. He just held her and told her it would be okay and that it was nothing to worry about since he will always be there for her and she would get through the pain. After opening up to J-Roc, Heaven stayed at his place for over a week.

 Heaven was so happy that he wasn't pressuring her into having sex with him even though she could tell he wanted to, just from the look in his eyes. She kept thinking "should I take this to the next step or is it too soon? Will I like it?" She was driving herself crazy, but one thing was for sure. She was catching strong feelings for him. The next day he came home with Chinese food. They ate, it was a nice candle lit dinner. He was giving her those glances that gave her butterflies. The next thing they knew, they were kissing and touching. Heaven put on some music from her phone, some classic R. Kelly and it seemed like one thing led to another. She & J-roc made love all night long. She told him that he was her first . J-Roc replied:

" I love you so much, Heaven. You don't have to ever worry about being hurt again, my baby. "

She just smiled and felt so good to hear those words. She was finally feeling loved again after everything she's been through in the last several months.

Heaven woke up the next day. The first thing she did was to call her friend, Tiffany.

"Oh my God, girl. I had sex with J-roc last night, and it was so good. I'm really starting to fall hard for him."

 "I`m happy for you. But be careful and take things slow. I heard a lot of bad things about J-roc in the streets and I know you already had a terrible year losing your parents to a violent crime."

 Tiffany just wanted her friend to be okay. She knew Heaven is at a really vulnerable place in her life. But she also was glad to see Heaven smiling and happy again. What both girls don't know is that J-roc also has a dark past and a few secrets that Heaven doesn't know about yet. Although J-roc is very nice, kind and sweet to Heaven, he was once in a long-term relationship with a girl. Their relationship was very toxic. The word on the streets is that J-roc was once arrested for domestic violence because the girl used to always provoke him and steal his money. Still, that wasn't an excuse to put his hands on her. If you were to look up J-Roc`s real name, Jimmy, he has a record for a couple violent crimes including assault, weapons, disorderly conduct and domestic violence. One of his exes says she has photos of him from that charge. She had two black eyes, busted lips, a few scrapes and a punctured lung due to severe punches. You would think that if a person did this to a woman once, then he probably could do it again. Heaven didn`t know this about J-Roc but she knew he had a history of dealing with the wrong kind of people. It's probably only a matter of time before she finds out the truth, because everything always comes to light in a relationship. It's probably best if J-Roc was upfront and told Heaven the truth about his past. It's always better to hear information from the source itself than to find out later from somebody else. But hey, Heaven is still head over heels about J-roc . Things are moving so fast she doesn't really know anything personal about him or about his past. It might have been better if she had got to know J-roc a little bit more before taking the relationship to the next level, but when you catch feelings for someone it is hard to see the bad in them or to even listen to anything negative someone might have to say about them.

One morning they were having breakfast when he opened his mouth and blurted out.

"My baby. Why don't you just move in with me? I'm in this apartment all alone. Plus a nigga would love to wake up to that pretty face every morning."

Heaven giggled with a big smile on her face from ear to ear.

"Are you sure? We are not moving too fast?"

"Hell no. We're doing just fine, baby girl. I told you. I got you and that's what I mean. You're going to be just fine. Why don't you give Tiffany a call and let her know I'm going to bring you over to her house so that you can go get all of your clothes and the rest of your belongings?

" Okay." Heaven said.

She was actually very excited to be moving. J-roc was so happy as well, walking around their apartment singing and dancing. You could see the joy in his face as the two of them began putting on their clothes so that they could drive over to Tiffany's house to get all of Heavens belongings. They got dressed, Heaven called up Tiffany on the phone.

" Hello."

"Hey, girl. What are you doing? Me and J-roc are going to head over to your house so that I can grab all of my things."

"What's going on? Wait. Why are you coming to grab all your things? Are you moving out? Did you find an apartment? Like we talked about a few weeks ago?"

" No. I'm moving in with J-roc. So are you at home right now?"

" Yes. I'm at home girl, but wait, rewind. You're leaving me and you're moving in with J-roc? She said with a concerning tone .

" Yes, I am. I just think this is the best move for me, at this time, girl. But one thing's for sure: I`m going to miss you and I will miss our movie and popcorn nights we had."

They both laughed a little.

"Yeah, okay then. I'll be over to your house in about 20 minutes. Boo, me and J-Roc were about to leave out the door in about five minutes but he can't find the car keys. Girl, I swear he loses the darn keys every other night." She laughed out loud.

" Well, okay said Tiffany. Just call me when you guys are pulling up. I'm here at the house waiting on you. If I find some bags I will start putting your things in them, I'll get your small pink Victoria Secret bag and put all of your lingerie and your hygiene personals in it, all nice and neat for you, my friend.

"Okay, cool. Thanks so much. Thanks for everything else you`re such a good friend to me. Definitely one of a kind. I don't know what I would have done without you, girl. You have been there for me every step of the way, with my parent's death ,the funeral and my brother's trial coming up very soon. Most definitely with giving me a roof over my head. When I had nowhere to go or know where to turn to you were there! I'll miss you so much."

" I miss you as well. At least J-roc only stays 20 minutes away from me. That means you could still come and visit me all the time."

" I agreed but we will have more privacy over here when you visit me. At your house, your mom was always in our business, checking up on us, seeing what we were doing."

"Yes, you're right and I'm so happy for you. I think J-roc might be the right guy for you. He has it going on for real. His own car, his own place, his own money. You kind of hit the jackpot, girl. I'll see you shortly, girl. I got everything all packed up and ready for you downstairs by the front door."

" Okay, we will be pulling up soon. "

"Okay, that's fine. I'll go ahead and unlock the front door."

Once heaven and J-roc pulled up at Tiffany's house, Heaven got out of the truck and began to walk up to the front door.

"Hey, do you need my help with the bags, baby?" said J-Roc.

"No, that's okay. I got it. Besides, it's just light bags anyway. And one of them is my small little pink Victoria's Secret bag with my personals inside. Thanks for asking me though, baby."

He gave her a big old smile, then while she was in the house, he jumped out his big black F-150 truck and ran up to the front door quickly, without heaven even seeing him. He was moving so fast and surprised her when she came back out the front door with her bags. J-Roc stood there with both hands held out, reaching for Heaven`s bags. They both laughed.

"Hey, I thought I told you I had it, baby."

" I know you did but... What type of gentleman would I be if I let my sweet, little baby girl carry some bags? I don't care if it was only one bag. I got them baby. No girlfriend of mine will be carrying anything. As long as I'm around!"

Both girls giggled.

"Awww, that's so sweet. I love the way you treat my girl. She's so lucky to have you."

"Yes. I am truly blessed and a very lucky girl."

Tiffany said goodbye to Heaven, then she hugged her friend while J-roc carried her belongings to the truck.

" Okay, that's everything. I miss you already. Make sure you call me later, girl. After you get all unpacked and settled at your new place. Good luck with everything and be sure to tell J-roc I got my eye on him. He better treat my friend well. "

"Okay, I'll tell him . I'll give you a call later, once I'm unpacked and settled in."

They headed back to his apartment. Once they got back, home J-roc took Heaven`s bags into the house and told her he had a few money moves to make and kissed her on the cheek.

"Hey, hold on. What is a money move? "J-roc turned back at heaven smiling.

"Oh baby, I meant to say a few business moves. I just have to go by a few of my partner's houses to go over some business with them and pick up these couple dollars. They owe me, I won't be long though. Baby, as matter of fact while we're on the subject… I forgot I got one of my dudes coming to pick up this package. I'ma need you to handle it for me, baby. You think you can handle it for me? If not, I can wait and take care of it myself. I'm just trying to hurry up and catch my other dude before he jumps back on the road. He has to go to Detroit to tie up some loose ends."

"Okay, that's fine baby. Just tell me what it is that you need me to do."

 He goes to the back room and comes back out with a package.

"All you have to do is give him this package and he's going to hand you $600, after that lock the door behind him and don't answer for anybody else . I'll be back in a few hours. My guy`s name is JT."

"Okay." Said Heaven as she kissed J-roc on the lips and locked up behind him.

Heaven was sitting on the couch watching one of her favorite TV shows- Love and Hip Hop Atlanta. The package was sitting in front of her, on the living room table. Heaven began to grow curious. She never asked J-roc what was in it or what he even sold because she didn't want to seem nosy or make him feel uncomfortable. But after 30 minutes passed she said to herself : "What the hell it can't hurt to take a little peek into the package!" She had always seen J-roc with lots of cash. She wanted to know what it was that he was selling so Heaven grabbed the package and opened it up to look inside.

She saw a white looking powdery substance with a kind of shiny sparkle in a clear plastic baggie and inside the bag. It was a drug called cocaine, on the streets it has a few nicknames : Coke, powder or clam. Heaven hurried and put it back in the package as J-roc had it and sat back to wait for his friend, JT. Heaven was a little frightened due to what she saw on movies and she heard in stories that people tell about what cocaine does to people. All she kept thinking about is the fact that she had fallen in love with a drug dealer or as her friends would say, with a d-boy . But Heaven was too blinded by the love and strong feelings she had grown for J-roc. She just kept telling herself maybe he's only doing this for a short time, maybe he didn't have a choice. whatever it was she decided

to stand by her man's side, through whatever. Then she heard a knock at the door.

"Who is it?"

"It`s JT."

" Coming!" Heaven said, she then opened the door.

"You must be the <oh so special, Heaven>. I heard many good things about you."

She smiled and said "nice to meet you", gave him the package, he gave her 600 dollars as he was leaving. He told her to tell j-roc good looking out and to hit him up.

"Okay. Bye !" Heaven said as she locked the door. Her heart was beating fast. She was sweating and very nervous. She had never thought in a million years That she would be doing an actual, real life drug deal for someone she loved."

"Wow! That was very different and unique."

Heaven locked up for the night, went to the fridge and grabbed some leftover lasagna, poured herself a glass of grape Kool-Aid and walked up the stairs to her and J-rocs bedroom. Sat down on the bed and thought about it.

"So this is how he is making all this money: off of selling this powder white stuff."

Heaven wasn't familiar with any kind of drugs until she moved in with J-roc and she started helping him sell his cocaine when he was away from home because he didn't want to miss a sale. She remembered when her brother and his friends used to experiment with different drugs, but her brother Devon had never exposed Heaven to anything. He would always tell her he didn't want that for his baby sister. She thought to herself" but look now : he is arrested and up for trial in just a few short days and our parents are murdered". Tears formed around her eyes, and she shook her head.

No, it can't be true. No, no. No, I can't believe my life right now."

Instantly her cell phone started ringing. It was J-roc.

"I'll be home in about 30 minutes, baby."

"Ok hurry. I really need to lay with you tonight. I'm just really emotional . "

"Okay. I'll be there soon."

Then she hung up the phone, laid back on the bed and shut her eyes.

As the day's grew closer to Devon Gates Smith final`s court date, emotions were all over the place. It's now been almost 5 months since their parents murders and Devon is facing possibly the death penalty for the double homicide . Poor Heaven is so lost, hurt and confused. More than anything, she wants to support her brother at court, but she still doesn't fully know the whole true story behind Devon's involvement in their parents murder. There are still so many unanswered questions that just don't add up.

Devon sits in jail also filled with pain, regret and guilt. Even though it wasn't him that pulled the trigger of the gun that night, he still blames himself .If he would have never started running with those guys or even sold his soul in the first place, then both of his parents would still be here today.

Now, the day has come. Devon sits nervously in cuffs and shackles at the long, wood table in the courtroom in front of honorable Judge Paul Simmons. His hands were sweating so much as he looked around the almost packed courtroom. He put his head down in shame and walked towards his sister with an almost blank look on his face. Heaven gave Devon a kind of half smile and put her hand up with a small wave. Heaven looked for an empty seat, she noticed a few familiar faces. One of the faces she noticed was the light skinned girl with blond dyed hair, the one her and Tiffany got into a fight with at the club, who also had threatened her about her brother snitching. Heaven's noticed her stomach was even bigger than the night when they had the altercation. They locked eyes for about 10 seconds, then Heaven quickly turned away.

She also noticed to the far right, all the way in the back of the courtroom, two boys. They were the same boys Devon was hanging with during the week leading up to their parents' murders. She felt the boys giving her a look of suspicion . Heaven locked eyes with the two guys, one of them gave her a nasty smirk and then held his fingers up to his mouth like he was signaling her to be quiet. Heaven then turned her head away , she quickly found a seat towards the front of the courtroom .She was sitting closer to Devon's table. She then noticed Devon having a stare-off with the same two guys, almost if something was up with the three of them.

The Honorable Judge Simmons came in. That's when everybody in the courtroom got up and then set back down . The court began. Heaven's heart was pounding. A mile beats per minute. She thought it was going to jump out of her chest . The judge started reading off Devon's charges: which were two counts of first-degree murder. He also mentioned that it would be a premeditated murder since there was a robbery at the time. That's why Devon could get the death penalty if he's found guilty of the charges. Heaven is so scared and confused. She started to cry, a nice old lady sitting next to her then handed her a tissue.

"Thank you. "

She told the little lady in a red dress sitting next to her.

"You're welcome, dear."

The judge asked Devon.

"How do you plead to the charges - two counts of premeditated murder and home invasion with intent to harm others?"

Devon then enters a not guilty plea.

Everyone in the room started chatting and whispering after Devon made his plea. The judge banged down his gabble and yelled.

"Silence!"

Once the courtroom settled back down and everybody got back quiet, Heaven noticed those same two guys who have been giving her and Devon nasty looks got up in a angrily manner, storming out of the courtroom almost as if they were in a hurry and they were only there to see if Devon would plead guilty or not. Heaven had a bad , almost scared kind of feeling about those two . She shook her head and said to herself" I wonder if Devon knows anything about those two guys ..Hmm" As hard as it would be for her to face her brother, she needed answers. She decided that after the court ended she would call on Monday and try to set up a visit with Devon for the first time since he's been locked up.

The trial came to an end. It was very emotional. The room was jam-packed with friends and co-workers of both Nevaeh and Daniels Gates Smith. In the back of the courtroom, Heaven spotted her best friend Tiffany - she didn't even realize was going to be there today. She smiled knowing she had at least one person in there who had her back and showed her support. That meant a lot to Heaven who was feeling sad and physically and emotionally drained. Now that Devon entered a not guilty plea, Heaven felt lost, lonely and hurt knowing that now she had to look forward to an extended murder trial. Heaven wiped a few more tears from her face and thought to herself.

"Devon couldn't have killed our parents. He just couldn't. "

Judge Paul Simmons ordered Devon to rise and repeat his plea. Since this was the final pretrial he set a date, two weeks from today and dismissed everyone from the courtroom.

Heaven locked eyes with her brother with a blank, frightened look on her face as two deputies escorted him out the courtroom back to jail. Devon walked away in shackles, escorted by guards. When he passed heaven he whispered "I love you Heaven, you know I couldn't have done this. You know me I didn't do it but it's still my fault" in a soft voice. Heaven just stared at him as deputies ordered him to keep walking.

" Hey Smith, no talking!

Heaven started walking making her way out of the courtroom. Her friend Tiffany was waiting for her at the door, they were standing in the hallway outside the courtroom. Tiffany looked at Heaven and held her arms out. She could tell her friend had been crying and needed a big hug , she hugged her best friend as tight as she possibly could . The two of them just bust out crying together .

" Oh my God, Tiffany. He couldn't have killed them. He just couldn't .I'm so hurt right now. I don't know what to do."

"It's going to be okay. We will get through this and we will find out what really happened that night. I'm here for you, girl. I got your back. What we need is a nice big glass of wine right now."

Heaven smiled at Tiffany as she wiped her tears saying yes.

"You read my mind.. Let's get the hell out of here."

" Yes, let's go. "

Heaven and Tiffany both walked out the courthouse together holding hands as they both went to carry on the rest of what seemed like a very long, emotional and confusing morning at the courthouse.

CHAPTER 5

The next morning Heaven and j-Roc woke up and smoked an early blunt. Then drove to McDonald's to grab some breakfast. When they got back to the house J-roc told Heaven that he needed her to stay home all day again and help him out by selling a bag of coke.

"You know, I'll do anything for you. But where will you be?"

"Just got to take care of a few things. So I need you, please baby."

Heaven frowned, hesitated and said:

"Okay, as long as you bring me back something good to eat tonight. "

"Thanks, baby. You've been so helpful since you moved in. I love you girl. I won't be too long. I will be back before it gets too late. I promise."

J-roc had only been gone for an hour and the first customer was knocking . She opened the door and eyed an old man up and down.

"What do you need?"

"Let me get a 40 bag of that."

Heaven weighed up some of the drugs, filled up a bag with it and quickly got the old man on his way. Not too much longer after that a familiar face pulled up in the driveway, it was JT the same friend of J-roc's. His real name was Jovontae . Heaven had met him many times to handle drug business but he was always around a lot, showing up at the house and hanging with J-roc. They were technically like best friends. Because both of their names started with J, they called themselves the J Brothers. They were even trying to start a rap group together- that annoyed Heaven so much.

JT hopped out his car and comes in the house with an aggressive loud tone asking Heaven:

"Where is my man J-roc and why is he never here every time I come to grab some goodies?"

Heaven gathered herself and responded.

"Don't worry about all that. He's gonna be gone until later tonight. Now. What do you need JT? "

"Okay, beautiful. Relax. Just asking but weigh me up a halfy of that good good. Ima count this money, baby."

Heaven weighs it up as he asked and gives it to him. He smirked at her and said:

" Keep up the good work. When I see him I'll let my brother J-Roc know how you're doing and holding it down."

Heaven looked back at him agitated.

" What is that supposed to mean ?"

"No, chill. I'm just fooling around. I might bump into him out in traffic. That's all."

Heaven slammed the door at the thought of JT talking about her with J-roc. She immediately called him and got no answer. She waited a minute and then called him again. Still no answer. Heaven started to worry: why did JT say that? A couple of moments later her cell phone started to ring. She heard J-Roc`s voice on the other end of the phone.

"What's up, baby? You called." Heaven shouted back in the phone.

"Where are you? Your so called brother, friend, whatever came over here being disrespectful."

" What you talking about?"

"JT came and grabbed some of that coke talking about he will holler at you for me. That's why I've been calling you to make sure you're okay because he gave me a bad feeling earlier."

 J-Roc laughed.

" Pay no mind. It's just my man`s JT fooling around. I saw him a little earlier and told him to stop by and grab that half. That's why he made that comment but me and him are supposed to make this drug run later to grab some product for a low price. So I won't be back home as early as I initially thought."

Heaven groaned.

"What do you mean?"

" I need you to hold it down for me, baby. Don't be mad. Plus we need the extra money."

Before she could finish her sentence a knock at the door made her jump. She could hear a lady say over and over: "Are you home? I really, really need a hit of that good stuff. Hey, are you home?"

"I think one of your fean tweeks is here."

" Okay, go ahead and take care of that . I'll call you before I make this four and a half hour ride. "

They hung up. Instantly ,Heaven thought to herself "that doesn't sound right". Then hurried and answered the door. The lady on the other side of the door rushed in immediately. Heaven yelled at the lady.

 "Don't just be walking up in my house. Like you ain't got no sense. What do you need?"

She looked the lady up and down. The lady wore raggedy clothes, was really skinny and wreaked of a very strong smell of drugs. Heaven knew that this lady was definitely a tweaker, which is someone who will do anything to get their next high no matter the cost. Heaven repeated her question and in an even higher tone of voice "what you need ?"

"Chill out. J-Roc knows me. I got some money. I need three grams of the good stuff you got here. He let me bust down to make sure it's smacking and I`m satisfied before I leave. You can ask him- it's just our routine."

 Heaven shook her head in uncertainty.

"I don't know about all that. "

"It's cool. "The lady responded. "Just call me auntie easy. That's what everybody in the hood calls me. "

Heaven wondered why in the world would they call her that. Then she chuckled to herself as if she then understood what the name meant. In the meantime, the lady sniffed a couple lines of J-roc`s product , took the rest and left.

Heaven was so disgusted. She closed the door behind the lady.

" This process is so annoying. I don't like dealing with all these random people, but the money sure is nice!"

She counted up all the money she had made that day: about nine hundred and fifty dollars.

"Wow. I'm so close to one thousand dollars already. This is some quick cash for sure."

Heaven walked up to a room to put the money up with the rest of J-roc`s stash. The stash had money, drugs and jewelry in it. She noticed a familiar looking silver 38 revolver sticking out in another box in the closet, near his usual stash spot. She took one look and feared that he had a firearm in the house . She closed the closet and left the room.

Heaven had no idea how scary her night was going to become. It was a quarter past midnight, Heaven was exhausted. She plopped down on the couch flipping through the channels when her cell phone started ringing. It was J-roc.

"What's good baby? How was your day? Did we make big money today?"

"You ain't making nothing!" Heaven joked . "But when are you going to get home? I miss you, and I'm starting to get sleepy. "

"Well, unfortunately, we are just now getting ready to leave. About to go grab this package from Sacramento. So it will take me about four to five hours till I get done and back home at the crib."

Heaven smacked her lips.

" Well, I guess I'm just going to sleep then."

"Don't wait up!"

She hung up and grabbed another glass of Kool-Aid from the fridge, went upstairs to the bed and jumped in. She started looking for a movie for about 10 minutes and then turned on something random right before she dozed off into a sleep.

She was asleep for about an hour when thunder and heavy rain woke her up. Heaven was always afraid of the rain since she was younger, but especially now that her mom and dad were killed on a rainy night it made her even more terrified to be alone. She tried to call her friend Tiffany and got no answer, her phone went straight to voicemail.

This situation had her nerves and anxiety at an all-time high. She turned on a light as laying in total darkness was giving her the creeps. The rain thudded loudly against the house and it only seemed to get louder after each ferocious roar. She hopped out of the bed and decided to take a nice hot shower to calm her nerves. She looked at the time and saw it was almost 2:00 a.m. J-roc should be home soon.

Heaven thought she heard a noise downstairs.

"What's that?" She blamed the wind outside.

She stared down over the top of the stair banister into the living room and thought she seen a shadow like figure going into the kitchen

"Heaven get a grip. You are totally spooking yourself out."

She ignored her fear and finished her journey to the bathroom. She walked in and flicked the light on and started her shower. Got out of her booty shorts and tank top, jumped into the water and started letting the shower sprinkle down her body.

She lathered up some shampoo and began to wash her hair.

"I just need to really relax. It's been such a long night. I'm just ready for it to be over."

She finished washing up her body, got out the shower, then started to dry off. Then walked over to the mirror and glared into it and thought of the myth of one of her favorite horror movies of all time.

"I wouldn't dare say his name five times on a night like this!"

She turned away from the mirror as quickly as she could. She still could hear the rain pouring down outside and the thunder sounded as if it was even louder than before. Heaven wrapped her towel around her and went downstairs to warm up some leftovers. She just couldn't shake how creepy this night was. She was trying to do anything to take her mind off of it. So maybe eating will help- she thought.

She made her way past the living room to the fridge. She bent down to look in it for the leftovers and then jumped in shock as she heard the TV in the other room turn on by itself with the volume turned up on max. It was so loud. She ran to the other room scared to death.

"How's the TV on by itself?"

She thought maybe it had to be a timer or something. She eagerly turned it off and before she could head back into the kitchen, she heard a familiar voice that gave her instant chills down the back of her spine.

"Hey Heaven, you got something I want and something I need and I'm here to take both."

Heaven spun around to see the grinning face of JT.

"What the fuck you doing in my house this late at night?"

Heaven got even louder.

" I hope this is not one of the J-rocs corny jokes. Where he at?"

" Oh, don't worry about that ! "JT Snapped back at her loudly then laughed. "He's out in Sacramento. Like we planned."

Heaven was extremely worried and so confused at this point.

I'm here for 50 bands.. J-roc told me all about the 50 thousand dollars he got stashed away here and I've been waiting for the right moment to make this move happen and tonight was the perfect night." JT laughed again. "Actually, you're over there looking very fuckable in that towel so I think I'll help myself to your goodies as well."

He looked her up and down like she was something to eat. Then plunged right at her, Heaven tried to run but he was too quick. He grabbed her arm then hit her in the back of the head with his pistol. She fell hard on the floor and passed out. Everything was a blur . Heaven felt her body being touched in ways she didn't want to be touched. She felt violated even though she was unconscious.

She could still feel the act of her being MOLESTED.

When Heaven woke up and regained her consciousness, she was tied to a chair in the living room, fully naked and exposed.

"Wake up, Sleeping Beauty!" JT said with a sarcastic voice." My man J-roc better appreciate you because you really had some good, tight pussy. I enjoyed that. Now tell me where the money stash is so I can go about my way."

Heaven started to cry.

"Why have you done this to me? I don't know anything. Just let me go and get out of here."

" I will once I get what I came for and you're going to tell me exactly where it is. If you don't I'm going to kill you. I'll count to three. I have already wasted too much time with you. I kind of got distracted when I came and seen you had nothing but a towel on."

Then he chuckled to himself and started counting: one, two… before he could say three Heaven shouted.

"It's in the back closet in the upstairs bedroom. You can take it or just please let me go."

JT ran up the stairs.

"Thanks for the info. I'll be out of your hair. "

A few moments later heaven could hear him upstairs in the bedroom rambling through the closet. She felt so disgusting and she had so much rage because of what just happened to her body. She tried to break herself free. But to no avail. She was tied up too tight. A few minutes later Heaven heard her phone start to ring.

"Where is it?"

She wondered. Then she looked around the room. "There it is". She noticed the phone reflection on the TV stand .

"J-roc must be trying to get a hold of me. Nobody else would be calling me this late."

Her cell phone rang two more times. Then she heard her text alert go off. JT suddenly came running back down the stairs in a joyful mood.

" I got that money. "He sang so proud of himself . "These Pockets going to be a lot better after today. I'm about to bounce out then and leave you."

Before he could walk out he heard Heaven`s phone go off. It was another text coming through. He grabbed the phone up and read the text out loud.

It said "get out the house now Heaven, my dude JT is up to something shady. He sent me on a fake drug run to get me out the city. But as soon as I found out I turned around one of my homies hipped me to what he was planning. He is not loyal like I thought . I hope you're okay ! Pick up the phone. I'm about to pull up any minute now, get out the house".

JT finished reading the text. Then looked directly at Heaven.

"Damn this motherfucker trying to mess my plans up. So I guess you are coming with me for reassurance. I still got to stop at my house to grab my bags and stuff so I can get out of Dodge and leave the city."

Heaven yelled.

"No, please you said that you would leave after you got the cash you were looking for. You found it. So please just take it and leave!" JT shouted back.

" Stupid, little, ho. You heard me - now you coming with me for reassurance."

Then he yoked Heaven up and shoved her out the door.

" You drive." He screamed while pointing his gun at her again. "That way I can keep an eye on you, hurry up, get in and drive. We're going for a little ride and I got one stop to make."

 Heaven unwillingly got in the driver's seat and started up JTs vehicle. He jumped in the passenger seat and aimed his gun directly at her.

" Now drive and don't try anything stupid. " He demanded. She obeyed his orders and started driving the car slowly.

"You can drive faster than that. I don't live too far from here. Just four or five more streets. That way!"

Heaven could not do anything but listen and follow his orders because she was terrified for her life and she really believed he would shoot her if he needed to. Once they reached his street, Heaven felt a little relieved. The morning was still dark and there were no cars on the road. It has to be about 4:30 in the morning.

"You see that small house on the left coming up? You can pull in that driveway." JT demanded . Heaven was just about to do as she was told when another vehicle turned around the corner at top speed. You could hear the tires screeching , the car made a ferocious turn, coming down the street towards them at full speed.

"Who is that ? JT yelled out loud.

Heaven squinted in the rearview mirror. It took her a few seconds to notice the familiar truck charging towards them.

" It's j-roc. "She said out loud. She was so happy to know it was him coming. Then she heard three wicked bullet shots go off. One of the bullets shattered the back window of JTs car.

"Oh shit. He's shooting. What the fuck? Drive now!"

JT Yelled again.

" I said drive or I will shoot you right now!" Heaven hesitated.

"But he doesn't know I'm with you. " She shouted back "That's why he's shooting at us."

JT started shooting back towards the J-rocs truck.

" I don't care. Drive!"

Bullets started flying. Heaven floored on the gas and the car instantly sped off. As she drove as fast as she could she thought to herself:" There is no way J-roc knows I'm in this car with JT. He would not be shooting at us both like this" then she heard JT yell.

"Hurry. Hurry, turn right there. He's gaining on us."

Heaven made a very sharp right turn then continued to drive like a crazy woman. They were going 90 miles per hour now. She could not believe she was stuck, driving this car during their shootout. There was a red light coming up.

"No, don't stop, keep driving right through it. "

J-roc was gaining fast. It seemed like he was driving even more crazier than she was. "If only he knew I'm the one driving." She thought to herself. "Maybe I can alert him somehow" she heard a couple more gunshots ring out and she turned towards JT.

He looked back at her and shouted:

" ayeee focus on the road."

It was too late. Before heaven could turn back around, she went through a stop sign and collided with the back of another car.

" Oh no!" She screamed out as the car spun in an entire 360 then flipped five times before finally landing on its backside .Police sirens filled the sky they were so loud you could hear them coming from everywhere. Heaven felt pain and agony through her entire body and she could hear the sirens coming from everywhere- that's the last thing she could remember.

Will this be her last breath ? Everything went black. Heaven tried to blink but couldn`t. Was it the light from the police cars? No, it was a very bright white light- she was sure of it .

She thought she was dead - she started to hear a sweet kind voice .It was her mother Nevaeh calling her name over and over .

"It's okay, my angel you're okay. "

" Mom!" Heaven called out." I miss you so much. Where are you? Please Mom? I need you."

The lights went away and a hospital room came into focus . Heaven realized she was laying in a familiar hospital bed.

"Ouch, I can't feel my arm. Wait. Where is my left arm? I can't feel it."

She yelled for help then a woman rushed in her room.

"You can't feel your arm. It's still there. It's just broken in a few places- that's it. We have had you sedated for the last day and a half . You were in a horrific car accident and very blessed to be alive. "

" I can't believe this!" she replied back to the doctor.

" Yes, it's been over 24 hours. "

The police has been in and out of the hospital waiting to speak with you. It seems that the man you were in the car accident with and the other guy who was chasing your car were both taken to jail on gun and drug charges. It seems your car hit the car of an off-duty officer and caused quite a bit of mayhem.

" Wait, I'm not under arrest, am I?"

Heaven looked up at the doctor very nervous.

"No, no."The doctor responded nicely." The young man who was chasing after the car you were in explained to the police that situation- he told them you had nothing to do with it and how you were kidnapped and held against your will and since he voluntarily turned himself in and told some very important information that had something to do with your brothers crime they cleared you from all charges . There`s some conditions though: you need to recover and you will have to leave the state and start fresh somewhere else."

Heaven felt relieved but also sad.

"Where will I go?" She thought about what the doctor had just told her about J-roc.

"He has been lying to me..." Heaven started thinking." He must of knew something more about my brother`s case and my parent`s murder. I just can't believe this. I'm not sure if I want to still be here. I'm just not sure life is worth living anymore."

The doctor interrupted her.

" Don't ever think or talk like that. You're still alive for a reason and you shouldn't take it for granted."

Then a voice on a loudspeaker called the doctor's name and she rushed out the room.

"I will be back. You need to get some rest."

Heaven laid in her bed, sore and aching. The phone next to her started ringing.

She reached with her good arm and answered it.

"Hello."

" Heaven! Are you? Okay? Where have you been? I've been trying to get a hold of you for weeks." It was Uncle Doug on the other end of the phone. "I thought you were dead. How are you?"

" Hey, uncle Doug, I guess I'm doing okay- lucky to be alive."

" That's what I'm hearing. Yes. Niece, I'm so glad you're fine. I heard the news and called the hospital directly. I have also spoke with the police and told them that it would be okay if you came down to West Virginia to stay with me and my wife and her daughter, Olivia. I told them I would take full responsibility over you since they are requiring you to leave the state after this last incident. Would you be okay with that for a while?"

Heaven responded in a sarcastic voice.

"I guess. Do I really have a choice at this point? "

"Well niece, you know, it could be far worse. Like you could be in jail right now or even dead."

She agreed. Uncle Doug spoke back in a stern voice.

" That's just what you need: a fresh start and you can definitely get it down here with us. So no worries get some rest and I will get all the arrangements together. I love you very much!"

Not even a minute after Heaven hung up the phone, a nurse walked into her room with a smile on her face.

"Miss Heaven Gates Smith? Congratulations!"

Heaven looked surprised and confused at the same time.

"For what?"

"The doctor has received back your results. You are pregnant."

Heaven almost had a full on anxiety attack.

" Wait! What ? How can this be? "She started crying, the nurse came over and started to hug and comfort her.

" It's okay, baby !" She told Heaven but she was so scared, sad and confused by this news .She could only wonder how this surprise would change and alter her life forever.